XAVIER LEFÈVRE

Five Sonatas
from *Méthode de Clarinette* (1802)
for clarinet and piano

Edited by
JOHN DAVIES and PAUL HARRIS

with a piano part realized by
DAVID ROWLAND

Grade 4   p. 11

Grade 5   p. 16

MUSIC DEPARTMENT
_____

OXFORD
UNIVERSITY PRESS

OXFORD

UNIVERSITY PRESS

Great Clarendon Street, Oxford OX2 6DP, England
198 Madison Avenue, New York, NY10016, USA

Oxford University Press is a department of the University of Oxford.
It furthers the University's aim of excellence in research, scholarship,
and education by publishing worldwide

Oxford is a registered trade mark of Oxford University Press
in the UK and in certain other countries

13 15 17 19 20 18 16 14

ISBN 0–19–357551–5   978–0–19–357551–6

Printed in Great Britain on acid-free paper by
Caligraving Ltd, Norfolk

The reproduction on the cover shows a French clarinettist, *c.*1804, and is from an engraving in the
possession of John Davies.

Xavier Lefèvre: Three Sonatas, ed. Georgina Dobrée, is also available from Oxford University Press.

CONTENTS

INTRODUCTION

Jean Xavier Lefèvre (1763–1829) was born in Lausanne. He studied the clarinet with Michael Yost in Paris, making his debut as a soloist at the age of twenty. From 1791–1817 he played in the Paris Opera orchestra and was principal clarinet at the imperial chapel (later the royal chapel) from 1807. When the Paris Conservatoire was founded in 1795, Lefèvre was one of nineteen professors appointed to teach the 104 clarinet students. He held this professorship until 1824. His *Méthode de Clarinette* of 1802 was adopted by the Conservatoire and remained the standard tutor for the instrument for a considerable period. He made an important contribution to the development of the clarinet by inventing the $c\sharp'/g\sharp''$ key in about 1790. In addition to his *Méthode de Clarinette*, Lefèvre's compositions include seven concertos, six trios for two clarinets and bassoon, forty-eight duos for two clarinets, and seven sonatas for clarinet with a bass line.

Lefèvre's twelve progressive sonatas comprise the final section of the *Méthode de Clarinette*, published by the Paris Conservatoire in 1802. The title page reads:

MÉTHODE / *DE CLARINETTE* / PAR X. LE FEVRE / Membre du Conservatoire de Musique et Prem.^re Clarinette de l'Opéra / ADOPTÉE PAR LE CONSERVATOIRE / *Pour servir à l'Étude dans cet Établissement* / . . . / Gravée par Mme Le Roy / A PARIS / *A l'Imprimerie du Conservatoire de Musique, Faubourg Poissonniere, N.° 152.* / AN XI.

The sonatas were originally published for clarinet with a bass line, and the piano realization given here is editorial. It is possible that this bass line was intended as a cello accompaniment rather than as a basso continuo, because of the occasional use of double notes which might seem to imply double stopping. Lefèvre's bass line has been adhered to in this edition, with the exception of seven instances where a slight alteration has been made in order to facilitate a more pianistic realization (see Critical Notes). Lefèvre's articulation markings are reproduced without alteration, though the engraver's inconsistencies are corrected and some additional slurring, marked editorially in the piano score, has been suggested. Editorial dynamics are placed in square brackets in the piano score. Beaming and stem directions have been modernized. The separate clarinet part does not include the differentiation between original and editorial markings that is in the score.

Articulation and ornamentation

In his introduction to the *Méthode*, Lefèvre states that 'the nature of the articulation is dependent upon the character of the music'. He goes on, however, to describe two main types of detached articulation, the *Piqué* and the *Coupé*. *Piqué* (which probably relates to the staccato dot) he describes as requiring a light articulation and he advises the player not to pinch the lips. *Coupé* (probably the wedge) he advises should be very evenly tongued with a lot of force. The third marking used by Lefèvre (♩♩♩) is not commented upon. In the opinion of the editors, notes marked with the staccato dot should be lightly articulated and played for about half their written duration. Notes marked with a wedge (♩) are to be more markedly detached with some degree of accentuation. Notes marked ♩♩ require a more gentle articulation with the minimum of separation.

Lefèvre's carefully ornamented clarinet line suggests that contemporary performers were not necessarily expected to add further embellishment. In this edition Lefèvre's ornamentation is reproduced exactly. Suggested editorial interpretations are shown in small notes above the stave. In the case of trills (where his marking + has been altered to the conventional *tr*), Lefèvre states in his introduction that they may begin on the upper or lower note. Players should use their discretion in the few cases where his intentions are not obvious. The editors have occasionally interpreted the appoggiatura, when occurring before a trill, as an acciaccatura.

JOHN DAVIES and PAUL HARRIS

CRITICAL NOTES

Sonata No. 1

3rd Movement: b.12 originally

bb.16–20 originally

bb.28–32 originally

Sonata No. 3

3rd Movement: bb.42–45 originally

Sonata No. 4

3rd Movement: bb.16–19 originally

Sonata No. 5

3rd Movement: bb.1–3, 9–11, etc. Ties removed in bass line.

bb.8 and 51 originally

Five Sonatas for Clarinet and Piano

from *Méthode de Clarinette* (1802)

Edited by John Davies
and Paul Harris
Realized by David Rowland

Sonata No. 1

JEAN XAVIER LEFÈVRE
1763–1829

Allegro moderato

Printed in Great Britain

OXFORD UNIVERSITY PRESS, MUSIC DEPARTMENT, GREAT CLARENDON STREET, OXFORD OX2 6DP

6

Rondo

Edited by John Davies
and Paul Harris
Realized by David Rowland

Sonata No. 2

JEAN XAVIER LEFÈVRE
1763–1829

14

Edited by John Davies
and Paul Harris
Realized by David Rowland

Sonata No. 3

JEAN XAVIER LEFÈVRE
1763–1829

Allegro moderato

CLARINET
Five Sonatas for Clarinet and Piano
from *Méthode de Clarinette* (1802)

Edited by John Davies
and Paul Harris
Realized by David Rowland

Sonata No. 1

JEAN XAVIER LEFÈVRE
1763–1829

Sonata No. 2

6

Sonata No. 3

Sonata No. 4

Polonaise

Sonata No. 5

Rondeau Pastorale

Sonata No. 4

Edited by John Davies
and Paul Harris
Realized by David Rowland

JEAN XAVIER LEFÈVRE
1763–1829

Polonaise
Allegretto

Edited by John Davies
and Paul Harris
Realized by David Rowland

Sonata No. 5

JEAN XAVIER LEFÈVRE
1763–1829

Allegro ma non troppo

Rondeau Pastorale

42

Printed in England by Caligraving Limited Thetford Norfolk